The Boxcar Children Mysteries

THE AMAZING MYSTERY SHOW

created by

GERTRUDE CHANDLER WARNER

Illustrated by Robert Papp

ALBERT WHITMAN & Company
Chicago, Illinois

Library of Congress Cataloging-in-Publication Data
is available from the Library of Congress.

The Amazing Mystery Show
Created by Gertrude Chandler Warner;
Illustrated by Robert Papp.

ISBN: 978-0-8075-0314-0 (hardcover)
ISBN: 978-0-8075-0315-7 (paperback)

10 9 8 7 6 5 4 3 2 1 LB 14 13 12 11 10

Cover art by Robert Papp.

For information about Albert Whitman & Company,
visit our web site at www.albertwhitman.com.

Contents

THE AMAZING MYSTERY SHOW

CHAPTER 1

A Game of Codes and Clues

"Wow!" cried six-year-old Benny. "Look at all the skyscrapers down there." The youngest Alden was staring out the window of the airplane.

"Philadelphia's a big city." Twelve-year-old Jessie smiled at her little brother. "It won't be easy tracking down clues."

Henry laughed a little. "It wouldn't be nearly as much fun if the mystery's too easy," he said. At fourteen, Henry was the oldest of the Aldens.

"We can do it!" said Benny. "We're good detectives. Right, Violet?"

"Right," ten-year-old Violet said. Then, with a worried frown, she added, "I know it's a game of codes and clues, but…we've never had cameras following us around before."

The four Alden children—Henry, Jessie, Violet, and Benny—were competing against another brother-and-sister team on "The Amazing Mystery Show." Grandfather, who had business in the city, had come along, too.

"Hey, I can see a river down there!" said Benny, pointing.

Grandfather nodded. "That's the Delaware River." He was looking out the window, too, over Benny's shoulder.

"I remember seeing a painting once," Henry said thoughtfully. "It showed George Washington crossing the Delaware."

James Alden nodded. "Yes, that's a famous painting, Henry," he told his oldest grandson. "Philadelphia's a modern city, but it's also a very old one. It goes all the way back to the Revolutionary War. In fact," he added, "this is where they signed the Declaration of Independence in 1776."

Benny's eyebrows shot up. "That was before I was born!"

"Even before *I* was born, Benny." Grandfather chuckled.

"Philadelphia is the home of the Liberty Bell," put in Jessie. "We read all about it at school."

"What's the Liberty Bell?" Benny asked.

"It's a big bell," Henry explained, "but it has a crack in it. That's why they don't ring it anymore."

"There's an inscription on it," Grandfather added. "RING LIBERTY THROUGHOUT ALL THE LAND."

"Cool!" cried Benny, catching on. "Know what else has a crack in it?"

The other Aldens looked over at their little brother. "What?"

"My cracked pink cup!" Benny said, making everyone laugh. "The one I found when we were living in the boxcar. Did you forget already?"

"We could never forget about your special cup, Benny," Jessie told him.

After their parents died, the four Alden children had run away. For a while, their home was an empty boxcar in the woods. But then their grandfather, James Alden, found them, and he brought his grandchildren to live with him in his big white house in Connecticut. Even the boxcar was given a special place in the backyard. The children often used it as a clubhouse.

As they made their way through the airport, Violet suddenly slowed her step.

Jessie seemed to read her thoughts. "Don't worry, Violet," she said. She knew that her younger sister was shy, and being on television would make her nervous. "When we start tracking down clues, you'll forget all about the cameras."

Violet gave her sister a grateful smile. Jessie always knew just what to say to make her feel better. "It *will* be fun exploring Philadelphia,"

Violet admitted, quickening her pace. "And I promised Mrs. McGregor I'd take lots of pictures." Mrs. McGregor was the Alden's housekeeper. She was staying at home with Watch, the family dog.

James Alden put a comforting arm around his youngest granddaughter. "I think it'll be a great experience," he assured her. "And I'm sure everyone on the show will make you feel at ease."

After flagging down a taxi, the Aldens headed for their hotel in the heart of Philadelphia.

"I sure hope they have good food around here," Benny remarked as they checked in at the front desk.

The young man behind the desk looked up, "Don't worry," he said, smiling at the youngest Alden. "Philadelphia's known for its great restaurants."

Henry grinned. "That's good," he said. "My brother's known for his great appetite."

This made everyone laugh—including Benny.

As they stepped inside their hotel suite, Grandfather nodded approvingly. "Looks like we'll be very comfortable."

"That's for sure!" said Violet, after looking around. "We even have three bedrooms."

"Henry and Benny can share one room," Jessie said. "Violet and I can share another. And there's one for you, Grandfather."

"We even have a kitchen!" Benny opened the refrigerator. "But no food."

"Don't worry," Henry said. "I just found a note taped to the bathroom mirror."

As everyone gathered round, Henry pulled up a chair and read the message aloud.

"Welcome to Philadelphia! Join us for dinner in the hotel restaurant at six o'clock."

Violet nodded as she glanced over Henry's shoulder. "It's signed by Hilary Griffin."

"Who?" Benny said.

"Hilary Griffin," Violet repeated. "The producer of 'The Amazing Mystery Show.' Grandfather spoke with her on the phone."

James Alden nodded. "It'll be nice to finally meet her."

Jessie glanced at her watch. "We'll have just enough time to unpack before dinner," she said in her practical way.

The other Alden children looked at each other and smiled. They could always count on Jessie to be organized.

****

Inside the restaurant, a young woman wearing a blue dress and sandals hurried over to greet them. "You must be the Aldens!" she said, holding out a hand. "I'm Hilary Griffin."

"I'm James Alden," Grandfather said, shaking hands. "And these are my grand-children — Henry, Jessie, Violet, and Benny."

"It's very nice to meet you," Jessie said, speaking for them all.

"Come and join the Best family," Hilary said, leading the way to a long table by the window.

As everyone sat down around the table, Hilary introduced the Aldens to the other brother-and-sister team—twelve-year-old twins, Rob and Rosie, and eight-year-old twins, Tim and Tammy. They all had the same curly fair hair and freckles.

"And this is Fiona Best," Hilary added. She nodded towards a middle-aged woman with gray streaks in her dark hair. "The children's aunt."

Fiona forced a smile. "So...*you're* the Aldens, are you?" she said. Then she suddenly leaned forward as if about the share a secret. "I don't mean to alarm you," she told them in a whisper, "but my nieces and nephews are unstoppable."

"They're really good detectives," Benny praised. "We saw them on 'The Amazing Mystery Show.'"

"Which city?" Twelve-year-old Rob wanted to know.

Henry answered, "San Diego."

"Oh, that one." Rosie yawned. "We're won so many times, it's hard to keep track."

"That's so true," said Fiona, laughing. Then she began to tick off each city on her fingers. "Let's see now, they won in San Diego....in

Chicago…in Nashville…and in Boston. One
more win and they'll become—"

"Five-time champions!" finished Tammy,
holding up five fingers.

Rob nodded. "And that means we can take
part in the Tournament of Champions."

"That's right," Hilary said as she passed
around the menus. "The tournament's in
Hawaii this year."

"Can you imagine?" Fiona clasped her
hands together. "Honestly, I've always wanted
to visit Hawaii." She had a dreamy look in
her eyes.

Timmy put in, "We're *this* close." He held
his finger and thumb an inch apart.

"Oh, honestly!" Fiona waved that away. "It's
as good as done."

Grandfather looked up from his menu. "I
wouldn't be too sure about that," he said.
"My grandchildren are first-class detectives."

Fiona rolled her eyes. "Yes, I'm sure they're
real pros," she said, though it was clear from
her voice that she didn't think they were real
pros at all.

Henry squared his shoulders. "We *have* solved quite a few mysteries," he said, looking Fiona straight in the eye.

Fiona did not seem very happy to hear this.

"But we never solved a mystery in front of cameras," Violet added honestly. "That must be harder." She glanced at Jessie nervously.

Fiona caught the look. "Are you sure you're up to it, my dear?" she asked. Then she reached over and patted Violet's hand. "Honestly, it's not easy being on television. *I* certainly couldn't do it," she quickly added. "Not with all those people watching at home."

Jessie couldn't shake the feeling Fiona was trying to make Violet even more uneasy. She opened her mouth to say something, but Hilary spoke first.

"Let's back up a minute," she said with a frown. "There's no reason for anyone to be nervous. No reason at all."

"I wouldn't say that," Fiona mumbled. "Not really."

"Well, I *would*." Hilary sounded annoyed.

"The cameras won't be rolling all the time. Even our cameramen needs breaks." She looked over at Violet and winked. "Besides, most of the film ends up on the cutting-room floor. It's only a half-hour show."

Violet looked relieved to hear this.

After the waitress took their orders, Tim said, "I take my lucky penny everywhere." He fished a coin from his pocket and held it up. "See?"

"Guess what?" Benny said with a grin. "I take my cracked pink cup everywhere." Tim grinned, too.

Over dinner, Jessie turned to Hilary. "Working on a television show must be fun," she said.

Hilary's eyes sparkled. "I really love my job, Jessie," she said, helping herself to a roll. "And since every show takes place in a different city, I even get to travel." Then she added with a sigh, "I plan to enjoy it while I can."

Henry raised an eyebrow. "While you can?"

Hilary nodded. "You never know when a

show might be cancelled," she explained. "It all depends on the ratings."

Benny scrunched up his face. "The ratings?"

"That's the number of people who watch, Benny," Hilary explained. "If we don't get enough viewers, then the show's cancelled."

"And you lose your job?" asked Violet.

Hilary nodded again. "And so does everyone else who works on the show."

"From what I hear," put in Fiona, "the ratings have really shot up lately. Honestly, my nieces and nephews have taken the nation by storm."

"True enough," said Hilary. "Can the Best family become five-time champions? Everyone's tuning in to find out."

"Do you make up the codes and clues yourself, Hilary?" Grandfather asked over dessert.

Hilary shook her head. "We have a team of writers who come up with the mysteries," she said. "They do the research on each city," she added. "Then they decide where the three gold coins should be hidden."

"Cool!" said Benny.

"Speaking of the gold coins," said Hilary, "we'll be meeting in the hotel lobby in the morning. We'll give both teams the same clues. As soon as you find the first gold coin, come right back to the hotel."

It wasn't until the Aldens were heading for the elevator after dinner that Jessie realized something. Hilary hadn't mentioned what time to meet in the lobby the next morning. As she dashed back to the restaurant, Jessie noticed Hilary sitting at the table talking on a cell phone. Coming up behind the producer, Jessie couldn't help overhearing bits and pieces of the conversation.

"Of course, I don't like sneaking around," Hilary was saying. "Yes, but…what choice do I have? No, no…I'm telling you, I'll do whatever it takes."

When Hilary caught sight of Jessie, she quickly pocketed the cell phone. "Oh!" She looked startled, as if she'd been caught doing something wrong. "I was, um, just…

checking on a few things."

"I didn't mean to startle you," said Jessie. "We were just wondering what time to meet in the lobby tomorrow."

"Oh, right," said Hilary. "We meet at nine o'clock sharp." The producer seemed unable to look Jessie in the eye.

As Jessie headed back to the elevator, she wondered just what Hilary had meant about sneaking around.

CHAPTER 2

Round One

"Where is everybody?" Benny said as he looked around the hotel lobby the next morning.

Henry glanced at his watch. "We're a bit early."

"Well, you know what they say," said Jessie. "The early bird catches the worm."

"Then I guess that's us," said a voice behind them. "We've been here for ages."

The Aldens turned to see Fiona coming into the lobby—with the four Best children close behind.

"We just dashed into the gift shop for a second," added twelve-year-old Rosie, as they sat down on a long leather couch.

Tim looked over at Benny. "Can you guess what's in my pocket?"

Benny grinned. "Your lucky penny?"

"Right!"

"I've got my lucky cup, too," Benny told him.

Fiona frowned. "You're not here to make friends, Tim." She gave her youngest nephew a little nudge. "You're here to win."

Jessie glanced over at Henry. She could tell by the look on her brother's face that he was thinking what she was thinking. What's wrong with making friends and trying to win?

Just then, a teenaged boy in a baseball cap poked his head into the lobby.

"Aren't you the kids from 'The Amazing Mystery Show?'" he asked, staring wide-eyed at the Best twins.

"Yup." Rob was beaming as he nodded his

head. "That's us, all right."

"Wow!" The teenager hurried over. "Can I get your autograph?"

"No!" Fiona made a shooing motion with her hand. "I won't have these children mobbed by fans."

The boy in the baseball cap walked away, his shoulders slumped.

Jessie glanced around. *Mobbed by fans?* Nobody else seemed to be paying any attention to the Best family.

"Honestly!" Fiona shook her head. "I suppose that's the price of fame," she added with a sigh. She was still shaking her head as she walked over to a table by the window. "These must be for us," she said, holding up some travel brochures and street maps. "Let's take a look at them while we're waiting, shall we?"

"Are you sure Hilary won't mind?" Violet asked as Fiona handed out a street map and a handful of brochures to each team.

"Honestly!" Fiona rolled her eyes. "Of course she won't mind."

At that moment, Hilary stepped into the lobby. She was chatting with a middle-aged man wearing jeans and a T-shirt. A younger man—about Hilary's age—strolled in behind them. He was tall and slim, with curly dark hair. Both men were carrying television cameras.

"Good morning!" Hilary said in a cheery voice. Her smile suddenly vanished when she caught sight of the maps and brochures. "How on earth did you get those?"

"Actually, we just helped ourselves," Fiona said. "Is that a problem, Hilary?"

Hilary did not look pleased. "I always give those out myself."

"Oh?" Fiona seemed surprised to hear this. "I didn't realize that."

"Well, what's done is done," Hilary said, forcing a smile.

Jessie and Henry exchanged puzzled looks. If Hilary always gave out the maps and brochures, why did Fiona act so surprised?

"I have a few more hand-outs," Hilary

told them. She gave each team a large thermos of lemonade, paper cups, and an envelope filled with dollar bills.

"Wow!" Benny's jaw dropped. "Is all that money for us?"

Hilary nodded. "You'll need it for lunch and transportation."

"Especially lunch," Benny said with a grin.

This made Henry smile. "Benny's middle name is food," he teased.

Hilary smiled, too. Then she gestured towards the middle-aged man. "This is Mike," she said. "He'll be with the Best family again. And Andy with be with the Aldens."

The young cameraman was leaning against the wall. He waved to the Aldens, and they waved back.

"Mike and Andy will get everyone ready for the day," Hilary told them.

"This won't take long," Andy said, after shaking hands with each of the Aldens in turn. "We just need to get you set up with microphones."

Benny's eyebrows shot up. "We'll be

holding microphones?"

"Nothing to hold, Benny." Andy held up a small recorder about the size of a wallet. "We'll clip this onto the back of your shorts. You'll soon forget you even have it on."

But Violet didn't look so sure. She was still nervous about being on television. How could they ever forget their words were being recorded?

"Nobody will even see them under our T-shirts," Benny remarked.

"That's the whole idea, Benny." Andy winked at the youngest Alden. "We don't want the folks at home to see our television equipment."

As soon as everyone had been equipped with microphones, Hilary handed each team a small wooden box.

"The clues inside these boxes," she told them, "lead to the hiding place of the first gold coin. You'll have until five o'clock today," she added. "Best of luck!"

With that, both teams headed for the door, with the cameramen close behind.

Outside, the Aldens set off in one direction, the Best family in the other. When Jessie spotted an empty bench by the bus stop, she sat down with the box.

"Hurry, Jessie," Benny pleaded. "Open the box, okay?" The youngest Alden was bobbing up and down with excitement.

With Andy's camera rolling, Jessie lifted the lid of the wooden box. Inside, they found a note, some cloth stars, and three spools of colored thread—red, white, and blue.

Jessie read the note aloud: "*Cats at play will show the way.*"

"Cats at play?" Benny echoed. "What's that all about?"

"You got me," said Henry.

"Thirteen," Jessie said, after counting the white stars. "Thirteen stars and three spools of thread. How weird is that?"

"I was just thinking," said Violet. "I'm not sure about the thread and the stars, but I have a feeling we should head for the zoo."

Benny looked confused. "The zoo?"

"I think I know what Violet means," said

Henry. "Lions and tigers are cats."

"And the zoo has lots of lions and tigers," Benny cried, suddenly catching on.

Violet was flipping through the brochures. "Here's a picture of the Philadelphia zoo." She held it up to the camera as Andy gestured to her. "I think it's worth checking out."

But Jessie wasn't so sure. How did the zoo fit in with the other clues—the spools of thread and the thirteen stars? Still, she didn't have any better ideas, so they decided to give it a shot.

"Keep your eyes open," Jessie said later, as they peered out the window of the bus. "We get off at Walnut Street."

"Don't worry, Jessie," said Benny, who was sitting beside her. "I'm a good detective. I always keeps *both* eyes open."

Sure enough, Benny was the first to spot Walnut Street. When the bus slowed to a stop, everyone hopped off. But something didn't seem right.

"I don't get it," said Henry, glancing

around. "This isn't a zoo—it's a park."

"I don't get it, either," said Jessie. "According to the map, the Philadelphia zoo should be right here."

The other Aldens exchanged puzzled looks. Jessie was the best map-reader in the family. It wasn't like her to get directions wrong.

Benny looked over at the cameraman. "Do you know where we are, Andy?"

"Sorry, Benny," Andy shrugged a little. "It's against the rules for me to help in any way," he said. "I wouldn't want to give Hilary an excuse to fire me."

"Would she really do that?" Violet asked in disbelief.

Andy nodded. "I'm afraid we don't exactly get along."

Violet was surprised to hear this. Andy and Hilary were such nice people. Why didn't they get along?

Just then, a woman pushing a baby buggy came along. "Excuse me," Jessie said to her. "Do you know how to get to the Philadelphia zoo?"

"The zoo?" The woman's eyebrows shot up. "I'm afraid you're way off course." After fishing around in her purse, she pulled out a pen and a pad of paper. "You're in Washington Square right now," she told them. "The zoo is in Fairmount Park." She drew a quick map and handed it to Jessie.

"We're not even close to the zoo," Jessie said, after thanking the woman. "I don't understand it." She was shaking her head as she stared at the hand-drawn map.

"Philadelphia's a big city, Jessie," Violet pointed out, as they headed for the bus stop.

"And we've never been here before," Benny added.

Henry nodded. "I bet visitors get lost all the time."

"I suppose," said Jessie. Still, she couldn't shake the feeling that something wasn't quite right.

****

"Camels!" Benny cried as they followed the tree-lined walkway at the zoo.

Henry, Jessie, and Violet hurried over to

look at the strange animals with the long
faces and the humps on their backs. Andy
turned the camera toward the camels, then
back to the Aldens.

"They're called ships of the desert," Henry
noted, as he read the information on a sign.

Benny gave his brother a questioning look.
"Ships of the desert?"

"Camels travel over oceans of sand,"
Henry explained, "so people call them ships
of the desert."

"Oh, I get it," Benny said. "Just like ships
travel over oceans of water."

"You catch on fast, Benny," Henry said.

"We did a unit about camels at school,"
said Jessie. "They can bite and spit."

"Bite and spit?" Violet raised her
eyebrows. "They don't look like they have
bad tempers."

"They can't be that bad," said Henry. "Not
if visitors can go for a ride." He pointed to a
sign that read: CAMEL RIDES.

"Do we have time?" Benny asked. He
looked at his older brother.

"Not if we want to find that gold coin," Henry answered.

"It should be just up ahead," Jessie said, checking out the map of the zoo. "The Big Cat exhibit, I mean."

"The zoo's a great place to hide a gold coin," Benny remarked, as they continued on their way. "Right, Jessie?"

"Right," Jessie said, trying to sound positive. But she was still convinced the thirteen stars and the spools of thread were important clues. She wasn't so sure they were really pointing the way to the zoo.

Andy and the four children threaded their way through the crowds to the Big Cat exhibit. Violet gasped when she caught sight of a tiger swimming in the water. "Oh, how beautiful!" she breathed.

"Tigers like swimming," Jessie stated. "See how he's using his giant paws to glide along?"

They soon spotted a jaguar snoozing in the sun, a lion beside a fallen tree, and a snow leopard climbing over the rocks. They were so interested in the wild cats, they forgot all about the gold coin for a while. It was Violet who finally remembered.

"The hiding place must be around here somewhere," she said.

"Oh, right!" Jessie smacked her forehead with the palm of her hand. "Let's split up," she suggested. "That way we can cover more ground."

Henry and Violet went one way, Jessie and Benny went the other. They kept a sharp eye out for the gold coin. But, after searching every inch of the walkway around the exhibit, they came back empty-handed.

"Looks like we struck out," said Violet.

"Never mind," said Jessie. "It was worth a shot."

"What now?" Benny asked, his shoulders slumped.

Henry looked at his watch. "It's almost lunchtime. I vote we head back," he said. "Didn't Grandfather say something about a park near the hotel?"

Jessie nodded. "Franklin Square," she

recalled. "Grandfather said we could get hot dogs there."

"Let's go!" Benny brightened. "What are we waiting for?"

"Andy," Henry said, scanning the crowds. "He was standing right here a little while ago."

"I noticed a gift shop nearby," said Violet. "Maybe he went to buy a souvenir."

"Could be," Jessie said. "Let's head over that way."

"Let's buy something for Mrs. McGregor while we're here," Violet said as they stepped inside.

"How about a coffee mug?" Henry suggested, as they browsed around the crowded shop.

Violet nodded. "I like the one with the giraffes on it."

"So do I," said Jessie. "Let's get that one."

While Violet and Jessie waited in the checkout line, Henry and Benny went outside. "Hey, isn't that Andy?" Benny asked.

Henry looked in the direction his brother was pointing. Sure enough, the young cameraman was standing in the shade of a tree, his back to them. When the children got closer, they realized he was talking on a cell phone. They caught some of his words.

"I'm telling you, I had to make the switch," he was saying. "Look, what choice did I have?"

Henry and Benny exchanged puzzled glances. Why did Andy sound so upset?

CHAPTER 3

The Storyteller

As soon as they got to Franklin Square Park, the Aldens made a beeline for a food stand. Henry ordered a hot dog and soft pretzels. So did everyone else—including Andy.

"Grandfather says Philadelphia is famous for its soft pretzels," Benny told the man behind the counter.

"Your grandfather's right," the man said. "You folks from out of town?"

Jessie nodded. "This is our first trip to Philadelphia."

"Well, there's a mini-golf course in the park if you're interested." The man placed the hot dogs and pretzels on the counter. "It's pretty cool," he added. "There's a miniature landmark on every hole—like the Liberty Bell and Independence Hall."

"Cool!" Henry squirted mustard over his hot dog. "Maybe we'll come back later in the week."

Jessie was glancing around for a place to eat. "There's a spot over there," she said, jerking her head in the direction of a huge bench.

"Somebody's sitting there, Jessie," Benny pointed out. "A lady in a costume."

"That's a storytelling bench," Andy informed them. "The city hires actors to dress up in costumes and tell stories about the early days in Philadelphia."

"Sounds like fun," said Jessie. "We can eat our lunch and hear a story."

The young woman in the long gown and white cap looked up from her sewing as they walked over. "I'm Caroline," she said, greeting them with a smile. "I was hoping you'd join me."

"What a pretty design," Violet remarked, after everyone said hello. She was admiring the woman's delicate stitches.

"I'm making a small tablecloth," Caroline told her. "I decided to add a border of blue cornflowers. Of course, I'm not as skilled as Betsy Ross," she added, "but I do my best."

"Betsy Ross?" The name sounded familiar to Jessie. "Didn't she sew the first American flag?"

"Nobody knows for sure." Andy wiped some mustard from the corner of his mouth. "But Betsy Ross usually gets the credit."

Caroline nodded. "According to the story," she told them, "it was George Washington who asked Betsy to sew the first American flag."

"That'd take forever," said Benny. He held out his cracked pink cup while Henry poured the lemonade. "To sew fifty stars and all those stripes, I mean."

Caroline shook her head. "Actually, Betsy

only sewed thirteen stars—one star for
every colony."

"What's a—" Benny began.

"Colony?" Henry knew the question
before his brother even asked it. "That's
what the first states were called," he said.
"Back when the settlers first came to
America."

Caroline nodded. "There were only
thirteen colonies back in the days of
the American Revolution. That's why
there were only thirteen stars on the first
American flag."

Thirteen stars? Jessie glanced over at
Henry. She could tell by the look on his face
that he was thinking what she was thinking.
Wasn't that the exact number of stars in the
box of clues?

Andy caught the look. In a flash, he
swallowed the last bite of his hot dog and
started filming again.

The storyteller went on to say that Betsy
Ross was a seamstress and a good friend
of George Washington's. But there was no

proof she actually sewed the first American flag.

After thanking Caroline, Jessie was anxious to talk to her sister and brothers. "That was a real stroke of luck," she said, as they tossed napkins and empty containers into a trash can.

"What was, Jessie?" Violet wanted to know.

"You're thinking about the thirteen stars in the box of clues," guessed Henry. "Right, Jessie?"

"Exactly!"

"Of course!" Violet put a hand over her mouth in surprise. "Then the clues are pointing to the first American flag."

"Got to be," said Jessie. "Even the spools of thread are red, white, and blue."

"Just like the flag!" cried Benny. Then he gave a happy twirl all around.

But Henry was having second thoughts. "One problem," he said. "What about the cats at play?"

"I'm not really sure what that's all about," admitted Jessie.

Violet's mind was racing. "Unless…"

"Unless what, Violet?" Henry asked.

"Unless the clues are pointing to Betsy Ross." Violet started flipping through the pages of a travel brochure. "I knew there was a picture of the Betsy Ross House in here," she said, thumping a finger down.

The other Aldens gathered round to take a look at a narrow brick house with a thirteen-star flag out front.

Henry said, "I think you're on to something, Violet."

Benny was quick to agree. "I bet that's where we'll find cats at play!"

"And it's open to tourists," Violet informed them.

"We can walk to it from here," Jessie told them, after a quick look at the map. "Chestnut Street isn't far."

Benny broke into a run. "Let's find that gold coin!"

****

"That can't be the Betsy Ross House," Violet said a little later. "It's too big."

For a long moment, the four Aldens stared in puzzled silence. The two-story brick building set back from Chestnut Street didn't look anything like the picture in the brochure.

While Andy filmed from a distance, Jessie sat down on a nearby bench. She unfolded the map to take another look. "Where did I go wrong?" she asked.

The other Aldens looked at each other in bewilderment. How could Jessie get the directions mixed up again?

Henry sat down beside his sister. "Maybe we can figure it out together."

That seemed like a good idea. As Violet looked over her sister's shoulder, she noticed something strange. The landmark picture of the Betsy Ross House was peeling away from the map. On a hunch, she reached over and pulled on one corner of the picture. Sure enough, it was just a sticker. And it was hiding another landmark underneath!

The Aldens looked at one another. For a moment, they were too stunned to speak.

"We're at Carpenter's Hall!" Violet said at last.

Jessie pulled off more stickers. The Philadelphia zoo had been switched with Washington Square!

"Somebody covered up the real landmark pictures with stickers," Henry realized.

"You mean, somebody tried to fool us?" A frown crossed Benny's round face.

"It sure looks that way," said Henry. "I guess he—or she—wanted to throw us off track."

Jessie let out a sigh. "We wasted a lot of time trying to find our way around."

"It's not very nice to trick people," Benny said in a small voice.

"No, it's not," said Jessie, who couldn't help noticing that Andy had stopped filming.

"But who would do such a thing?" Violet wondered.

"I'm not sure who tampered with the map," Henry said. "But I think we should concentrate on one mystery at a time."

"Good idea," said Jessie, who was bending over the map again. "We've still got time to get to the Betsy Ross House. It's only a few blocks away."

Henry jumped to his feet. "Then let's go," he said. "We're not giving up that easily, are we?"

"No!" the others shouted.

With that, the Aldens set off lickety-split.

CHAPTER 4

Cats at Play

When the Aldens finally arrived at the Betsy Ross House, Andy said, "There's no filming allowed inside the house, kids. I'll wait in the courtyard."

Henry gave him the thumbs-up sign. "We'll meet you out there."

As the four children stepped inside the house, they breathed in the musty smell of the past. The narrow little house was filled with tourists, so they had to thread their way through the crowds as they went from room to room.

"It's kind of like walking through a haunted house," Benny said as they climbed the winding staircase.

"Don't worry, Benny," said Violet, who was a step above him. "Ghosts don't exist."

They looked for cats in the shadowy kitchen where herbs hung from the ceiling, and in the storage room piled high with boxes of fabrics. They looked for cats in the small parlor where portraits covered the walls, and in Betsy's bedroom with its four-poster bed. They even looked for cats in the workroom filled with the tools of Betsy's trade—thimbles, spools of thread, and fabric.

When the Aldens stepped out into the courtyard, Andy called out to them, "Any luck?" He was sitting at a small table in the shade of a tree.

"Zilch," Henry said as they pulled up a chair. "No sign of cats anywhere."

"It doesn't make sense." Jessie was shaking her head. "I was so sure we were on the right track this time."

"Speaking of time." Henry glanced at his watch. "It's running out fast."

"I've drawn a blank," said Jessie.

Just then, Benny caught his breath.

"What is it?" Jessie asked in alarm.

Benny's eyes were huge. They all looked over in the direction he was staring.

"Is that what I think it is?" Violet asked in disbelief.

Henry nodded his head. "Cats!"

Sure enough, a fountain in the middle of the courtyard was decorated with bronze cats!

As Andy started filming again, Jessie gave her little brother a hug. "What would we do without you, Benny?"

"I'm a pretty good detective, aren't I?" Benny beamed.

"They look so real," Violet said, as they hurried over to the fountain. She rubbed a hand over one of the bronze cats. "This one's dipping his paw into the water."

Jessie laughed a little. "This one's scratching his back against the fountain."

At that very moment, something caught Henry's eye. The others watched in amazement as their older brother stuck his arm deep into the water. When he pulled it out again, he was holding something in the palm of his hand. As he slowly uncurled his fingers, Jessie, Violet, and Benny gasped.

Henry was holding a gold coin!

****

"We won the first round!" Benny said for about the umpteenth time.

"We still have two more rounds to go," Henry reminded him. "Don't get too excited yet."

The four children had gone for a swim later that evening. Now they were sitting on the edge of the pool, dangling their feet in the water.

"I can't believe somebody tampered with our map!" Violet couldn't stop thinking about it. "Who would do such a thing?"

Benny had an answer. "Fiona."

Jessie looked at her little brother. "How can you be so sure?"

"Because she wants to go to Hawaii," Benny answered. "It's her dream."

"That's true," said Violet. "And she won't get there unless the Best kids become five-time champions."

Jessie nodded. "Fiona didn't look happy when we showed her the gold coin."

"She said it was just beginner's luck," Benny added.

"Fiona does have a motive," Henry said after as moment's thought. "But what about opportunity? I'm not sure she had a chance to tamper with the map."

"You're forgetting something, Henry," Jessie reminded him. "They got to the lobby before we did this morning."

"That's true," Henry said, backing down a little. "She could've switched the landmarks on the map while the twins were browsing in the gift shop."

Violet remembered something else. "Fiona made a point of handing out the maps," she said. "Maybe she wanted to make sure we got the mixed-up one."

"It's a pretty strong case against Fiona," Henry admitted. "But she isn't the only suspect."

The other Aldens looked over at him, puzzled.

"I think we should include Andy on our list."

"Oh, Henry!" cried Violet. "You don't really suspect Andy, do you?"

"I don't want to think he would do something like that, Violet," Henry said. "But we have to consider everybody."

"And we heard him on the phone," Benny said, lowering his voice.

"What are you talking about, Benny?" Violet wanted to know.

"I'm talking about when we were at the zoo."

Henry nodded. "He said something about making the switch."

Jessie didn't like the sound of this. Neither did Violet.

"Are you positive?" Jessie asked. She wanted to be sure.

Benny gave the water a splash with his feet. "We heard it with our own ears."

"Now that you mention it," Jessie said after a moment's thought, "Andy suddenly stopped filming when we were peeling the stickers off the map. Did you notice?"

Henry had thought nothing of it. Neither had Violet and Benny. But now they wondered about it, too.

"I bet he didn't want anyone to find out he'd tricked us," guessed Benny.

They had to admit it was possible. After all, the ratings had shot up since the Best kids had taken the nation by storm. And wouldn't the show be cancelled if the ratings went down? Andy would lose his job if that happened.

"You know," said Jessie, "there's somebody else we should consider."

"Who's that, Jessie?" Violet asked.

"Hilary."

"Hilary!" The others were so surprised, all they could do was stare at Jessie with their mouths open.

"But, Jessie," said Violet, "Hilary seems so nice."

"We all like her, Violet," said Jessie. "But she'll lose her job if the ratings go down."

"And she likes traveling to different cities," Benny recalled.

Violet didn't look convinced. "That's not much to go on."

"There's something else," said Jessie. "I overheard Hilary talking on the phone, too. She said she didn't like sneaking around, but she didn't have any choice."

"That does sound fishy," Henry admitted. "I think we should keep a close eye on all of them for now—Fiona, Andy, *and* Hilary."

The other Aldens were quick to agree. There was definitely something funny going on!

CHAPTER 5

The Two-Parter

The next morning, Hilary once again handed each team a thermos of lemonade, an envelope of money, and another small wooden box.

"This mystery will be a two-parter," she told them. "You'll need your best detective skills with you today."

"Honestly, that's a bit much!" Fiona suddenly snapped.

Hilary look puzzled. "What do you mean?"

"You know very well what I mean!" Fiona shot back, getting more annoyed by the minute. "There's *never* been a two-parter before. Never!"

"Well, there's a first time for everything," Hilary said quietly.

"But it's not fair to these children," Fiona said, gesturing toward her nieces and nephews. "It's not fair at all!"

That was the wrong thing to say. "The clues are the same for both teams," Hilary said in a hard voice. "There's no use rolling your eyes, Fiona. Everyone has an equal chance to…" Her voice trailed away as Fiona stormed out of the lobby.

The Aldens looked at each other in amazement. Why did Fiona rush out like that?

Hilary seemed caught off guard for a moment. But she recovered quickly. "You'll find a riddle inside the box," she went on, "that will lead to another riddle. If you figure out the answers to both, you'll—"

"Find the gold coin!" Benny blurted out. He sounded excited.

"That's right." Hilary smiled at the youngest Alden. "And you'll have until five o'clock to find it. So good luck to everyone!"

"Can you believe that?" Jessie said, as they headed outside. "Fiona just turned her back on Hilary and walked away."

"I guess she's worried," said Violet. "Maybe she thinks a two-parter will be too hard to solve."

"That doesn't excuse her for being rude to Hilary," Jessie insisted, as they sat down together on an empty bench.

Henry, Violet, and Benny waited expectantly as Jessie lifted the lid of the wooden box and pulled out a folded piece of paper.

"Read it, Jessie!" cried Benny. The youngest Alden couldn't stand to be kept in suspense.

With Andy's camera rolling, Jessie unfolded the note and read the riddle aloud.

> "*Up a ladder,*
> *down a pole,*
> *look for an arrow*
> *high and low.*"

"An arrow?" Benny's eyebrows shot up. "That's weird."

They were all lost in thought for a moment. Finally, Violet spoke up.

"Something just popped into my head," she said. "Do you think 'ladder' and 'pole' could be the names of streets?"

"I suppose it's possible," said Henry, although he didn't sound convinced. "We can check it out."

Jessie shook her head as Henry fished around for the map in the backpack. "Let's buy a new map," she suggested. "I don't trust that one anymore."

"Good idea," said Henry.

Violet pointed to the sign just behind them. "Why don't we try that store? It sells everything under the sun," she said. "At least, that's what the sign in the window says."

Benny was on his feet in a flash. "They'll sell maps for sure!"

As the children headed for the store, a woman with red hair suddenly dashed out the door. She almost knocked Benny over.

"Honestly!" she snapped.

"Are you okay, Benny?" Jessie asked as the woman hurried away.

"That lady wasn't very nice," Benny said in a small voice.

"No, she wasn't, Benny." Jessie put a comforting arm around him. "She didn't even say she was sorry."

"It's the weirdest thing," Violet said as they went inside the store. "For a second, I thought…"

"Thought what?" Jessie asked.

"Oh, it's nothing." Violet laughed a little. "I'm probably just imagining things."

"Wow!" cried Benny, glancing around at all the souvenirs lining the shelves. "They really do sell everything under the sun." There was everything from Betsy Ross dolls to Philadelphia ball caps. Violet even spotted a rack of postcards.

"Let's buy one for Mrs. McGregor," she suggested.

Jessie was quick to agree. "That's a great idea."

While Violet and Jessie browsed through the postcards, Henry checked out the street maps, and Benny wandered around the store.

"They have so many," said Violet. "It's hard to choose."

Jessie held up a postcard of Independence Hall. "How about this one?" she asked. "It's the building where they signed the Declaration of Independence."

Violet didn't answer. She was staring at another postcard.

"Violet?"

Violet suddenly snapped out of it. "Sorry, Jessie," she said. "Take a look at this postcard of the Fireman's Museum!" She sounded excited.

Jessie glanced from Violet to the card and back again. "Do you think Mrs. McGregor will like that one best?"

"I think *we'll* like this one best!" she said mysteriously. Stepping up to the counter beside Henry, she quickly added the postcard to his purchase.

"This store even has old-fashioned costumes!" Benny said as he joined them. "And all kinds of wigs."

"I wish we had more time to look around," Jessie said, smiling at her little brother.

"Do we have enough money to buy a souvenir?" Benny asked. He was pointing to the gold coins behind a glass case.

Henry glanced over. "Sorry, Benny," he said. "We really can't afford Betsy Ross coins. We might need our money for transportation and lunch."

"Oh, right." The youngest Alden let out a sigh.

"Never mind, Benny," Violet said, as they stepped outside. "I have something exciting to tell you."

"What's going on, Violet?" Jessie asked.

Violet answered by holding up the postcard. "It's the Fireman's Museum!" she cried, her eyes sparkling.

Jessie looked puzzled. So did Henry and Benny.

"What's going on, Violet?" asked Henry. He could tell by the look on his sister's face that something was up.

"Don't you get it?" Violet asked. Then she recited the latest riddle from memory. "*Up a ladder, down a pole, look for an arrow high and low.*"

Jessie's face lit up. "Firemen climb up ladders and slide down poles!" She gave her sister a high-five. So did Henry and Benny.

"Violet, you're a genius!" said Henry.

"Not really," Violet said modestly. Andy gestured to her and she held the postcard up to the camera. "When I spotted the postcard, it just popped into my head."

"We'll find that arrow in no time," said Benny. He rubbed his hands together with excitement.

"Good news," said Henry, who was already checking out the new map. "Looks like the museum's right here in the historic district."

With that, the Aldens set off with Andy. After a few blocks, Henry couldn't help noticing that Jessie kept looking over her shoulder. He could see that something was troubling her.

"What is it, Jessie?" he asked her.

"I'm not sure," Jessie answered. "I just have the strangest feeling somebody's following us."

"Somebody *is* following us," Henry pointed out. "Look!"

Jessie glanced back at Andy. His camera was propped up on one shoulder as he filmed from a short distance away. "Yes, I'm sure that's all it is," she said, smiling a little. Still, she couldn't shake the feeling there was somebody else was following them, too.

It wasn't long before they arrived at the Fireman's Museum—a three-story brick building with arched doorways for the fire engines to go in and out. While Andy waited in the sunshine, Henry, Jessie, Violet, and Benny hurried inside.

They found the museum filled with all kinds of old-fashioned fire equipment—everything from horse-drawn fire engines to antique axes. There was even a brass pole that went all the way from the first floor to the third floor. But they didn't have any luck finding an arrow.

Henry gave Andy the thumbs-down when they stepped outside again.

"I was so sure we were on the right track," said Violet. She let out a sigh as she sat down on a nearby bench.

Jessie poured lemonade into Benny's cracked pink cup. "It was a good try."

"But if we can't figure out the first riddle," said Benny, "how can we find the second one?"

Violet sighed again. "That's a good question."

"I just wish we—" Henry suddenly stopped talking in mid-sentence. His mouth dropped open.

Violet turned to her older brother. "What is it, Henry?"

"This is a one-way street!"

"What's wrong with that, Henry?" Benny wondered.

Henry pointed to a street sign beside the

Fireman's Museum. It was an arrow pointing one way!

The four children raced over to the pole with its one-way arrow on top. Andy was right behind them, his camera propped on one shoulder. Benny was the first to notice the message printed in yellow chalk on the pavement.

"What does it say?" he wanted to know. The youngest Alden was just learning to read.

Henry read the words printed around the pole.

> *"It makes no sound*
> *but its words ring true;*
> *crack this case*
> *and win round two."*

"I wonder what it means," Benny said.

"And where it's leading," added Jessie, tugging a small notebook and pencil from her back pocket.

While Jessie made a copy of the riddle, the others looked at each other, baffled. Even Andy walked back to the bench, scratching his head. Finally, Violet spoke up.

"One thing's for sure," she said, "this'll be a tough riddle to figure out."

"It's a real mystery," said Henry. "No doubt about it!"

CHAPTER 6

Quack, Quack!

The four children were still racking their brains when they stopped later in Franklin Square. They were sitting cross-legged on a shady patch of lawn.

"If something doesn't make a sound," said Benny, "how can it have words?"

"Books have words," Violet pointed out, as Jessie passed around the hamburgers.

"And they don't make a sound," added Henry.

Andy held up a hand as he unwrapped

his burger. "I thought you kids were taking a break from the mystery over lunch," he reminded them. "If you keep this up, I'll have to start filming again."

"You're right," Henry said, handing everyone a napkin. "A break just might clear our heads. Don't you think so, Jessie?"

Jessie nodded, but she was only half-listening. Her forehead wrinkled into a frown as she searched through the backpack. "It must be here somewhere," she said under her breath. As she held the backpack upside down and gave it a shake, maps and brochures tumbled out onto the grass.

"Something missing, Jessie?" Violet wondered.

"It's gone!" A look of concern crossed Jessie's face. "I don't understand it."

"What's gone, Jessie?" Benny wanted to know.

After a long pause, Jessie answered, "I'm afraid it's your cracked pink cup, Benny."

"What...!" The youngest Alden almost choked on his pickle.

"It couldn't just—disappear!" said Violet.

Benny had an opinion about this. "I bet somebody stole it."

"I doubt that, Benny," said Henry. "Who would anyone steal a cracked pink cup?"

"A thief!" said Benny. "That's who."

"We shouldn't suspect people," Violet said quietly, "unless we're certain it was actually stolen."

Henry had been thinking. "I have a hunch we left your cup back at the Fireman's Museum," he told Benny.

The youngest Alden brightened. "You really think so?"

Violet agreed. "Jessie poured you some lemonade," she recalled, "when you were sitting on that bench."

"We'll go back after lunch and check it out," Henry promised.

But Jessie wasn't so sure. She couldn't remember seeing Benny's cup on the bench. At least, not after they went to look at the one-way sign.

Still, as soon as they finished eating, the

little group went back to the Fireman's
Museum. But Jessie was right. Benny's
cracked pink cup wasn't on the bench. It
wasn't in the trash can. And it wasn't in the
museum's lost-and-found.

"It's gone," said Benny. He slumped down
on the bench, his chin in his hands. He
looked crushed.

Violet could feel her little brother's
disappointment. "Don't worry, Benny," she
said, sitting down beside him. "We'll check
in the lost-and-found again tomorrow."

As they headed back along the street,
Jessie was trying to think of something
cheery to say, but Henry spoke first.

"Guess what the detective duck said to his
partner?" he asked.

"What?" Benny gave his brother a
half-hearted smile.

"I hope we *quack* this case!" Henry said,
making them all laugh.

They laughed even harder when Benny
added, "I hope we find my *quacked* pink
cup!"

This got Jessie thinking. She tugged her notebook from her pocket and read the riddle aloud again. *"It makes no sound but its words ring true; crack this case and win round two."*

"The first part is the trickiest," Violet noted.

"That's true," Jessie agreed. "But I think there's a clue in the last two lines. Henry's joke gave me an idea."

"What are you getting at, Jessie?" Henry wondered.

"Benny's cup isn't the only thing in Philadelphia that's cracked."

Henry suddenly caught his sister's meaning. "The Liberty Bell!"

"Exactly," said Jessie.

"That's true," Benny said with a nod. "They can't ring it anymore because of the crack."

"But its words still ring true," Violet added.

Henry remembered the words: *"Ring liberty throughout all the land."*

"You think that's the answer to the riddle?"

Benny wondered. "The Liberty Bell?"

"I'm sure of it!" said Jessie.

When Andy stopped to answer his cell phone, Henry flattened out the creases on the street map.

"Here's the Liberty Bell Center," he said, tapping a finger on the map. "If we keep going, then—"

"That was the producer, kids," Andy cut in. "The Best family just arrived back at the hotel."

Benny's eyes widened. "You mean...?"

Andy nodded. "They found the second gold coin at the Liberty Bell Center."

The Aldens looked at each other in dismay. They had solved the riddles—but it was a little too late.

CHAPTER 7

Trick or True?

"First, we lose my cracked pink cup," Benny was saying, "and then we lose round two."

The four Alden children were heading down the street from the hotel. They were on their way to the photo shop after dinner that evening.

Violet stopped to drop their postcard into the mailbox. "We still have one more round, Benny," she reminded him.

"And you know what?" Henry added. "I

have a hunch we'll find your special cup,
Benny."

"I hope so," Benny said, as they filed into
the photo shop. "Hey, isn't that Andy?"

Sure enough, the cameraman was standing
at the counter, his back to them.

"Hi, Andy!" Violet said, coming up behind
him.

"Oh!" Andy was clearly startled to see
the Aldens. "I was…just picking up some
snapshots." Just then, a photo slipped from
the counter and fluttered to the floor. A
funny look came over the young man's face
as Violet bent to pick it up. "No, no, I'll get
it," he said, waving her away.

Before Violet had a chance to say
anything, Andy had slipped the photo back
into its envelope and dashed out of the
shop.

"What was that all about?" Henry
wondered. It was almost as if they'd just
caught Andy in the middle of something he
wanted to keep secret.

"I'm not sure," said Violet. She gave the

sales clerk her roll of film. "But things are getting stranger and stranger," she whispered behind her hand.

When they stepped outside again, Jessie turned to her sister. "What did you mean about things getting stranger and stranger?"

"I was talking about the photo," Violet said with a frown. "The one that Andy dropped."

"What about it?" Benny asked.

"It was a picture of Andy and Hilary," said Violet. "They were holding hands and smiling."

"That's weird." Jessie looked puzzled. "Andy told us they didn't get along."

"Do you think Andy lied to us?" Benny wondered.

"It sure looks that way," said Jessie. "But it doesn't make sense. If Andy likes Hilary, why would he want to keep it a secret? There's nothing wrong with having a crush on somebody. Is there?"

"No," Henry said, as they stopped at the light. "Not if that's all it is."

"You think there's more to it than that?" Jessie wondered.

Henry nodded. "Why else would he try to keep it a secret?"

"Do you think Andy's up to something?" Benny wondered.

"Yes," Jessie answered with a quick nod. "We just don't know what."

"It *is* suspicious," Violet admitted. "But I don't think we should jump to conclusions."

"I suppose you're right," Jessie said.

"You don't think..." Benny began.

"Are you wondering if Andy took your pink cup?" Henry asked his little brother. "I don't blame you. I've been wondering about that myself."

"But there's no reason for him to do something like that," Violet said. "Is there?"

"Somebody's working hard to make sure the Best kids become five-time champions," Jessie pointed out. "First, he—or she—tampers with the map, and then Benny's cup disappears."

"Somebody's trying to distract us," Henry concluded.

"Andy was in the right place at the right time," Violet had to admit.

"Maybe," Jessie said thoughtfully. "But I still can't shake the feeling somebody was following us today."

Violet and Benny were surprised to hear this. "Who do you think it was?"

"I can't be sure," Jessie said. "But I know somebody was there."

The more she thought about it, the more certain she was.

****

"Do you think it'll be another two-parter today?" Violet asked, as they had an early breakfast in their hotel suite the next morning.

"I guess we'll find out soon enough," Henry said as he poured himself another bowl of cornflakes.

"Don't forget," Benny reminded them, "we're checking out the lost-and-found at the Fireman's Museum."

"For sure," said Jessie.

"I forgot something!" The youngest

Alden pushed back his chair and raced into the other room.

As soon as Benny was out of earshot, Henry whispered, "I bought something last night." He reached into his pocket and pulled out a gold coin.

"Oh, it's the Betsy Ross coin!" cried Violet. "The one Benny wanted to buy."

Henry nodded. "I thought he might need some cheering up," he told them. "Just in case we can't find his special cup, I mean."

"Benny will love it," said Jessie.

Just then, Benny came back into the room. He was holding a drawing of his cracked pink cup. "This is for the lost-and-found," he said, "so they'll know what my cup looks like."

"That's a great sketch, Benny," said Violet. "I'm sure it'll help."

"I thought you might be anxious to see these, Violet," Grandfather said as he stepped through the door, a rolled-up newspaper under one arm. He handed his youngest granddaughter an envelope thick with photos.

"Oh, thank you, Grandfather!" Violet's face lit up. "I've been wondering how they turned out."

While James Alden read his newspaper on the balcony, the four children looked through the photos. "This is a great shot of Caroline," Jessie remarked.

Benny scrunched up his face. "Caroline?"

"The storyteller in Franklin Square," Henry reminded his little brother.

"Oh, right," said Benny. "This is a good one, too."

Jessie looked over at her little brother. "Which one is that?"

"The one of the giraffe munching on leaves." Benny held it up. "See?"

Henry glanced over. "You're becoming a wonderful photographer, Violet," he praised.

"Thanks, Henry." Violet gave her older brother a grateful smile. But she was soon frowning as she bent over another photo. "That's funny," she said. "I don't remember this place."

Jessie took a good look at the snapshot. It showed a brick building with a white steeple. "Oh, that's Independence Hall," she said, recognizing it from the postcard. "You know, where they signed the Declaration of Independence."

Benny looked confused. "But…we didn't visit Independence Hall."

"Probably just a mix-up," Henry concluded. "I bet we got somebody else's picture by mistake."

Violet was bending over the photo again. "That can't be."

"What makes you say that?" Jessie wanted to know.

"For starters, take a good look at the picture." Violet held it up for everyone to see.

Benny blinked in surprise. "Is that what I think it is?" he asked. The youngest Alden was holding a spoonful of cereal in midair.

Violet nodded. "It's your cracked pink cup, Benny."

Henry let out a low whistle. "What's it

doing on the lawn at Independence Hall?"

Jessie added, "And who took the picture?"

"Not us," said Henry. "That much we know for sure."

"Do you think this is somebody's idea of a joke?" Jessie wondered.

"Well, if it's *not* a joke," said Henry, "then it can mean only one thing."

"What, Henry?" Benny asked.

"It's some kind of clue."

"Back up a minute, Henry," said Jessie. "Are you saying we'll find Benny's cup at Independence Hall?"

Henry nodded. "That'd be my guess."

Benny was on his feet. "Then let's get it back!"

"Wait!" Violet held up a hand. "There's something weird about this snapshot. Did you notice?"

The others were instantly curious. "What are you talking about, Violet?"

"Don't you think the cup looks a bit strange?" Violet asked, without taking her gaze from the photo.

"Strange?" Benny looked confused.

Violet nodded. "It looks like a giant cracked pink cup!"

"What?" Henry laughed a little. "You're kidding, right?"

"Take a look, Henry." Violet passed the photo to him.

"Uh-oh!" Benny's mouth dropped open as he looked over Henry's shoulder. "What in the world happened to it?"

Sure enough, Benny's cracked pink cup was almost as big as the front door at Independence Hall!

"Maybe it's trick photography," Jessie suggested.

Henry was deep in thought. "Or maybe…"

"Maybe what, Henry?" Jessie wondered.

"Maybe the building's too small."

"Too small?" Benny looked confused. "That's even weirder."

"Not as weird as you might think." A slow smile spread across Henry's face. "I think I know where we can find Benny's cup!"

CHAPTER 8

Giants

"Where are we going, Henry?" asked Benny, as he tried to keep pace with his brother's long stride.

"Don't forget," Jessie added, "we're meeting Hilary in the lobby at nine o'clock sharp."

"Nothing to worry about," Henry called back to them as he led the way along the busy sidewalk. "It's not far."

Rounding a corner, Violet glanced up ahead. "Are you talking about Franklin Square Park, Henry?"

"You guessed it!" Henry was grinning as they crossed the street. "I have a hunch that's where we'll find Benny's cup."

"Grandfather says we're seldom wrong when it comes to hunches," Benny said, trying to catch his breath.

As the four children made their way into Franklin Square Park, Henry stopped to look around. "Which way now?" he asked, tapping a finger against his chin.

Henry looked first in one direction, then in another. A moment later, he sprinted ahead. Curious, the others followed. They made a loop around a huge fountain, then ran full-speed along a walkway. When Henry finally slowed to a stop, Jessie, Violet, and Benny turned to him in bewilderment.

"What are we doing here, Henry?" Jessie was panting as she peered through the fence at a miniature golf course. "We don't have time to play—"

"We're not here for a round of golf," Henry assured her. "Just to get Benny's cup back."

Jessie wrinkled her forehead. So did Violet and Benny.

"But…why here, Henry?" Benny wanted to know.

Seeing their puzzled faces, Henry said, "Remember what the hot dog seller told us the other day?"

"About the miniature golf course?" Violet questioned. "Is that what you're talking about, Henry?"

"That's exactly what I'm talking about."

"Hmm." Benny thought hard. "Didn't he say we should have a game while we're in Philadelphia?"

Henry nodded. "He said something else, too."

"Oh!" Violet's snapped her fingers as she caught his meaning. "He said there was a famous landmark on every hole!"

"That's right." Jessie nodded. "He even mentioned Independence Hall!"

Benny scratched his head. "You mean, they signed the Declaration of Independence on a miniature golf course?"

Jessie had to bite her lip to keep from laughing. "Not exactly, Benny," she said, as they walked over to the ticket booth. "It's just a copy—a miniature Independence Hall."

"That's why Benny's cup looked so big in the photo," Violet realized. "It was in front of a tiny building."

"We're out of luck." Henry pointed to the sign in the window of the ticket booth. It read: OPENS AT 10:00.

But Benny wasn't giving up so easily. When he noticed somebody in the booth, he tapped on the window.

The young man inside looked up in surprise. "We're closed!" he shouted.

"We lost something," Jessie shouted back. "Do you mind if we go inside for a minute?"

The young man opened the window. "I've already checked everything out," he said. "There was nothing left behind."

"Could we just take a quick look?" Violet asked in her soft voice. "It's something that means a lot to our little brother."

"Fine." The young man let out a sigh. "Just be quick about it."

"Wow!" Benny said, as they walked around the course. "I feel like a giant in this place."

"I know what you mean, Benny," said Henry, slapping at a mosquito on his neck. "It's like every landmark's been shrunk down to dollhouse size."

There was every landmark from Elfreth's Alley—a street lined with tiny shops and homes—to a miniature version of the Ben Franklin Bridge.

When they spotted the Liberty Bell on the eighteenth hole, Violet giggled. "It looks like you can putt right through the crack in the bell," she noted. "How funny is that, Jessie?"

But Jessie didn't answer.

"Jessie?" Violet gave her sister a little nudge.

"There it is!" Jessie cried. She pointed to a miniature landmark nearby. "That's Independence Hall."

They all turned to see a small brick building with a white steeple. "It sure looks like the building in the photo," agreed Henry.

"Then where's my special cup?" Benny asked as they hurried over. "That's what I want to know."

"It's here somewhere, Benny," Violet assured her little brother. But a part of her wasn't so sure.

"Maybe it's *inside* the building," Jessie suggested after some quick thinking.

"Let's check it out!" Henry was already kneeling down by the pint-sized building. He tugged gently on the front door and it swung open.

Everybody held their breath as Henry stuck his hand into the opening and patted all around.

"Anything there?" Benny asked in a hushed voice.

"Ta-daah!" cried Henry. When he turned around to face them, he had a cracked pink cup in his hand. Standing up straight, he held the cup out to his little brother. "I think this belongs to you, Benny."

The youngest Alden was all smiles as they made their way back to the hotel. "I'll never let it out of my sight again," he said. "Not ever!"

"One thing's for sure," said Henry. "Andy's looking more and more suspicious."

Jessie nodded. "I know what you mean," she said. "He certainly knew Violet was getting film developed."

"Maybe he went back to the photo shop this morning," Henry concluded, "and slipped an extra picture into our envelope."

"I don't think Andy's the nice person he pretends to be," Violet admitted reluctantly.

"Not if he was trying to distract us," Jessie agreed.

Henry added, "This time, his plan didn't work."

Benny agreed. "We found my cracked pink cup just like that!" he said with a snap of his fingers.

The Aldens looked at each other. Would they find the last gold coin just like that?

CHAPTER 9

The Strange Riddle

"Don't open the box just yet, Jessie," Andy was saying. "One more minute and we'll be set to go."

While the Aldens waited on an empty bench, Violet whispered, "Did you see Fiona's reaction when Benny walked into the lobby?"

Next to her, Jessie nodded. "She couldn't take her eyes off his cracked pink cup."

"It makes you wonder, doesn't it?" Violet sighed. "It's hard to know what's really going on."

"Are you ready now?" Benny called out to Andy. The youngest Alden was wiggling with suspense.

"Ready!" Andy called back, propping his camera up on his shoulder.

With a quick motion, Jessie flipped open the lid of the wooden box and removed a small sheet of paper. As she read the riddle aloud, the other Aldens leaned closer to catch every word above the noisy traffic.

> *"A kind of ship*
> *that never sails—*
> *it bites and spits*
> *and has a tail.*
> *What is it?"*

"I've never heard of a ship with a tail," said Henry.

"Or a ship that never sails," added Jessie.

The Aldens thought long and hard about the strange riddle. Benny was the first to break the silence.

"I bet Fiona bites and spits," he said with a frown.

"Oh, Benny!" cried Violet. "I know she's

not very friendly, but I don't think she bites and spits."

"She sure wasn't friendly to Hilary yesterday," Jessie recalled.

"Fiona's hard to figure out," put in Henry. "She doesn't even want the Best kids to make friends with us."

"I guess she doesn't place any value on friendship," Violet said with a shrug.

Benny's big eyes got even bigger. "That's it!"

The other Aldens looked over at him, puzzled. "What's it, Benny?"

"The answer to the riddle!" Benny almost shouted. "It's *friend*ship."

Jessie thought about this. "That's a good guess," she said. "But—"

"It doesn't bite and spit," Benny finished with a sigh.

"It doesn't have a tail, either," Henry pointed out.

Benny's face suddenly brightened. "A dragon has a tail," he said. "And it bites and spits fire, too!"

"That's true," said Violet, smiling a little. "But a dragon isn't a kind of ship."

That didn't stop Benny. "How about a ship filled with so many dragons that it can't even float?"

The others burst out laughing. "Keep trying, Benny," said Henry. He gave his little brother a pat on the back.

Andy suddenly spoke up. "How about we change location," he suggested. "That fountain in Franklin Square would make a better background. How does that sound?"

The Aldens thought it sounded just fine. Andy stopped filming as they headed for the park.

"It'll seem strange to go back to normal," said Violet. "Without a camera following us around, I mean."

"I know," Henry was quick to agree. "I can't believe this is our last day on the show."

Hearing this, Andy said, "Actually, it's my last day on the show, too."

The children stared at the cameraman in surprise.

"What happened?" Violet asked in alarm. "Was the show cancelled?"

"No, nothing like that," Andy told her. "I accepted a job with another station."

The Aldens all looked at each other, stunned.

"You're leaving 'The Amazing Mystery Show?'" Jessie could hardly believe her ears. "But...why?"

"I thought you liked working for the show," Benny said, looking confused.

"It's a great place to work," Andy was quick to say. "But there's one catch."

As if on cue, the Aldens asked, "What's the catch?"

"The show frowns on its employees dating each other."

"You're talking about you and Hilary, right?" guessed Violet.

Andy didn't deny it. "We had to keep it a secret or we'd lose our jobs," he confessed. "But I can't do that anymore," he added. "You see, I'm planning to ask Hilary to marry me."

"Oh, how sweet!" Violet said, a dreamy look in her eyes.

"I know how much Hilary loves working on the show," Andy explained. "So...I decided to make the switch."

Henry nodded his head in understanding. That's what Andy had meant on the phone. He wasn't talking about switching the landmarks on the map. He was talking about changing jobs.

Andy looked over at the children sheepishly. "I'm sorry for not being honest with you before," he said. "You must've wondered when you saw the photo of us together, Violet."

"I'm glad you told us," Violet said, as they drew near the fountain. "It explains a lot."

The Aldens looked at one another. They were each thinking the same thing. They could cross Andy off their list of suspects.

The four children turned their attention back to the riddle as they perched on the edge of the fountain. Andy, who was standing nearby, started filming again.

Henry read the riddle aloud one more time to refresh everyone's memories. "*A kind of ship that never sails, it bites and spits, and has a tail. What is it?*"

"I keep thinking we're close to figuring it out," Jessie added thoughtfully. "I just can't quite put my finger on what it is."

"What's the matter, Benny?" Violet asked when she heard her little brother sigh. "Thinking about something?"

Benny nodded. "I was thinking about putting through the crack in the Liberty Bell."

"We'll come back tomorrow and have a game, Benny," Henry said. "That's a promise."

"And we'll go for a ride on the camels," Violet added.

"Did you say"—Jessie paused—"camels?"

Violet nodded. "The ones at the zoo, Jessie. Remember?"

"Camels have tails...and they bite and spit," Jessie said slowly, figuring it out as she spoke. "And they're called—"

"Ships of the desert!" Henry cut in. "Ships that don't really sail."

Jessie's eyes were shining. "Guess where we're going?"

The others were ready with an answer. "To the zoo!" they all cried out.

Just then, something caught Violet's eye. A woman with curly red hair was sitting on a bench nearby reading a newspaper. She was wearing sunglasses with tortoise-shell frames. The woman was peering over her paper, staring at the Aldens.

Violet leaned closer to the others. "Let's get going," she whispered nervously.

With that, the Aldens headed for the bus stop with Andy close on their heels.

CHAPTER 10

The Show Goes On

A warm breeze was blowing when the Aldens arrived at the Philadelphia zoo. They could tell it was going to be a hot day.

"I just knew we'd figure out that riddle," Benny said as they headed along the tree-lined walkway.

Henry gave his brother a big smile. "It does look like we've got a real shot at winning."

As they rounded a bend, they caught sight of the camels. "Now, where's a good hiding place for a gold coin?" Violet said, glancing around.

"Let's split up again and check all around," Jessie said in her practical way.

Andy held up a hand. "Listen, kids, I'm just heading for the washroom. Don't find the gold coin before I get back, okay?" he added with a wink.

Henry laughed. "It'll take us a while to look around."

While Andy walked over to the washroom, the four children started their search for the gold coin. It wasn't long before Violet called out, "Over here!"

As the others hurried over to where Violet was standing under a tree by the side of the walkway. They watched as she reached into the hollow of the tree and pulled out a gold coin.

"Way to go, Violet!" Henry praised. He tucked the gold coin Violet handed him into his back pocket.

Just then Violet spotted something that made her gasp. "She followed us!"

"Who?" asked Henry, glancing around.

"See that woman standing by the water

fountain over there?" Violet said in a hushed voice.

"The one reading the map?" Benny asked. "I can't really see her face."

"She's just pretending to read the map," Violet said in a hushed voice. "This is going to sound a bit weird," she added, "but I think that's the same woman who was just at Franklin Square."

"Are you sure?" Henry asked in surprise.

"She has the same red hair and the same sunglasses," answered Violet, who had an artist's eye for detail.

"It could just be a coincidence," said Jessie. "Maybe she was planning to go to the zoo today."

"But she's watching us, Jessie," Violet insisted. "She keeps peeking over the map at us. And she was doing the same thing at the park."

"There could be a good reason for that," said Henry.

"Like what?"

"We're being filmed, Violet," Henry

reminded her. "That would make anybody curious."

Violet had to admit Henry had a point. Still, she had a hunch there was more to it than that.

"You know what would really be funny?" Benny piped up. "If it was the same woman who almost knocked me over. She had red hair, too."

"Now that you mention it," Violet said slowly, "it just might be the same woman."

"She didn't even say she was sorry," said Benny, who still couldn't get over it. "She just said, 'Honestly!' and hurried away.

"Fiona!" Violet suddenly realized there was only one person it could be.

The other Aldens looked over at Violet, puzzled.

Benny scrunched up his face. "Fiona doesn't have red hair, Violet."

"But she was coming out of a store that sells wigs," Violet pointed out. "Right?" She kept her voice low. She didn't want her suspicions picked up by the recorder clipped to the back of her shorts.

"They even sold *purple* wigs," Benny said, nodding his head up and down.

"Fiona really wants that trip to Hawaii," Violet reminded them, eyeing the woman uneasily.

Henry didn't look convinced. "Enough to wear a disguise and spy on us?"

"And steal my special cup?" added Benny.

Violet nodded. "I knew there was something familiar about the woman who almost bumped into Benny. But I couldn't figure out what it was," she said, "until Benny reminded me of what she said." Violet looked around at her sister and brothers. "What's Fiona's favorite expression?"

Jessie shrugged. "You've lost me, Violet."

"Her favorite expression is 'Honestly!'" answered Violet. "That's what she's always saying."

"You're right, Violet." Henry nodded his head slowly. "And it's an interesting theory, but—"

"It isn't enough to go on," finished Jessie.

Henry thought about this for a moment. Then he snapped his fingers. "I have an idea," he said as a foolproof plan flashed into his mind.

"What is it?" Benny wanted to know.

Henry made a big point of looking at his watch. "We've got lots of time," he said, his voice booming. "Let's take a look around the zoo." He fished the gold coin from his pocket and put it back into the hollow of the tree. "We can come back for this later."

"What if the Best kids find it before we get back?" Benny asked in alarm.

Henry waved this away. "Don't worry, they'll never find it."

"But, Henry," said Jessie, "how can you be so sure?"

"Just go along with me on this, okay?" Henry said without moving his lips. "I'll explain on the bus ride back to the hotel."

The other Aldens looked at each other. What was their older brother up to?

****

Later that morning, when the Alden

children were chatting with Hilary and Andy later that morning, the Best kids suddenly burst into the lobby.

"We did it!" cried Rosie.

Fiona and Mike stepped into the lobby behind them. "I knew they could do it," Fiona said, beaming.

"Do what?" Hilary looked confused.

"Become five-time champions, of course," said Fiona. "What else?"

Rob handed the gold coin to Hilary. "We found it in a hollowed tree."

"Near the camels at the zoo," Timmy added.

"I was just on my way back from shopping," Fiona explained, "when I spotted them racing down the street. Can you believe they won the third round before lunch?"

"No, I can't believe it," said Hilary. "You see, this isn't even one of our coins." She was shaking her head as she looked closely at it.

Fiona's smile faded. "What...?"

"Our coins have the name of the show on one side," Hilary explained, "and the number of the round on the other side."

"So?" Rosie shrugged.

"*This* coin has Betsy Ross on one side," said Hilary, "and the first American flag on the other."

"The Aldens already found the real coin," Andy informed them.

Rosie looked over at Fiona in surprise. "But, you said…" Her words trailed away.

The children caught the look. Hilary had seen it, too.

"What do you know about this, Fiona?" Hilary demanded.

"*Me?*" Fiona pointed to herself. "How would I know anything about it?" she snapped. "It's clear the Aldens have played some kind of trick on my nieces and nephews."

"We didn't play a trick," Henry said, his eyes never leaving Fiona. "We set a trap."

"A trap?" A look of shock crossed Fiona's face.

"We saw you spying on us!" said Benny, his arms folded. "You were wearing a red wig and sunglasses," he added, "but Violet knew it was you."

Henry nodded. "I just let you think I was putting the coin back into the hollow of the tree," he said. "But it was in my pocket all along."

Jessie added, "Henry actually put a Betsy Ross coin back in the hiding place."

Fiona gave an angry toss of her head. "I wouldn't know anything about that," she said. "I have nothing to hide. Nothing whatsoever."

"You switched the landmarks on our map," Violet said quietly. "We kept getting lost."

"And you stole Benny's cup to distract us," put in Henry.

Hilary looked from Fiona to the Aldens and back again. "Is any of this true, Fiona?"

"I told you it wouldn't work," Rob muttered.

"Rob, please!" Fiona gave her oldest nephew a warning look. "You're not helping matters."

"I think you have some explaining to

do," said Hilary, who was pacing around the lobby. "What do you have to say for yourself, Fiona?"

"Okay, okay!" Fiona held up her hands in surrender. "Maybe I did get a bit carried away," she admitted. "But I figured if my nieces and nephews won, it would help the show's ratings. What's wrong with that?"

"What's wrong with that?" Hilary looked horrified. "That's not the way to increase ratings, Fiona! Any hint of cheating would ruin the show."

Fiona shrugged. "My mistake," she said, forcing a laugh. "I was just trying to help," she added, trying to make light of everything.

"And get a free trip to Hawaii," said Henry, watching Fiona closely.

"You should be happy the Aldens won," Andy told Fiona. "Otherwise, your nieces and nephews would be forced to withdraw from the show."

"I can't believe it, Fiona," said Hilary, sounding more disappointed than angry. "I knew you were determined to win, but I had no idea you would stoop to cheating. What kind of example are you setting for these children?"

Fiona lowered her eyes and her face reddened. She sank down into a chair, looking defeated. After a moment's silence, she began to speak. "When I heard that the Aldens were first-class detectives, I started to get worried," she said. "I found some landmark stickers in the gift shop," she went on. "It started me thinking."

"So you stuck them to one of the maps," Jessie guessed. "Only, you put them where they didn't belong."

"That's why you handed out the maps and brochures that first morning," Violet realized. "You wanted to make sure we got the mixed-up map."

Fiona didn't deny it. "But you won the first round anyway," she said with a sigh, "so I bought a wig and sunglasses and followed you."

"Then you stole my cracked pink cup,"

Benny said accusingly.

"I didn't mean any harm," said Fiona. "After all, it was just an old cup."

"It wasn't just an old cup to Benny," Jessie said.

"It was more than that," added Violet. "A lot more."

"I'm truly sorry," Fiona said in a small voice. "I've done a lot of things I'm not very proud of."

Fiona told her story quickly. When she saw the Aldens going into the photo shop, she decided to leave them a snapshot clue to the whereabouts of Benny's cup. The next morning, she went to the photo shop and pretended to be picking up the photos for Violet. Instead, she added her own picture to the envelope.

Fiona looked over at the Aldens. "I realized what good detectives you were," she said, "when you found the cup so quickly."

"So you decided to follow us again," Violet concluded.

Fiona nodded as she went on with her

story. She followed the Aldens to Franklin Square. When she heard them talking about going to the zoo, she told her nieces and nephews. She had spotted them checking out the wooden animals on the carousel nearby. Then she drove out to the zoo in her rental car and waited for the Aldens to arrive. By a stroke of luck, she watched Henry put the gold coin back into its hiding place. At least, she thought it was the gold coin. She waited for her nieces and nephews to arrive at the zoo. Then she told them where to find the gold coin.

"It seemed like the perfect plan," said Fiona. "Especially since I made sure Mike didn't see me talking to my nieces and nephews." She let out a long, weary sigh. "I just didn't count on the Aldens setting a trap."

Hilary shook her head. "I think it's time for the Best family to pack their bags and leave."

Looking truly regretful, Fiona walked slowly from the room. The Best kids were close behind her.

Jessie had a question for Hilary. "What did you mean when you said you didn't like sneaking around and that you'd do whatever it takes?"

"Oh, you heard that, did you?" Hilary was smiling. "It's not what you think."

"You were talking about Andy," guessed Violet. "Weren't you?"

"Why, yes," said Hilary, who seemed surprised that Violet knew that. Turning to Andy, she added, "I accepted a job on another television show. Now we won't need to sneak around anymore."

Andy threw his head back and laughed. "Great minds think alike," he said. "I accepted a job on another show, too."

Violet clasped her hands together. "How romantic!"

Andy looked over at the Aldens. "By the way," he said, "we need to shoot some film of you kids actually finding the last gold coin at the zoo. I hope that's okay."

"Sure," said Henry. "We never get a chance to wrap up a mystery twice!"

"Can we have lunch first?" Benny asked. "Mysteries always make me hungry."

"Oh, Benny!" Jessie giggled. "Everything makes you hungry."

At this, even Benny had to laugh.

GERTRUDE CHANDLER WARNER discovered when she was teaching that many readers who like an exciting story could find no books that were both easy and fun to read. She decided to try to meet this need, and her first book, The Boxcar Children, quickly proved she had succeeded.

Miss Warner drew on her own experiences to write the mystery. As a child she spent hours watching trains go by on the tracks opposite her family home. She often dreamed about what it would be like to set up housekeeping in a caboose or freight car—the situation the Alden children find themselves in.

While the mystery element is central to each of Miss Warner's books, she never thought of them as strictly juvenile mysteries. She liked to stress the Aldens' independence and resourcefulness and their solid New England devotion to using up and making do. The Aldens go about most of their adventures with as little adult supervision as possible—something else that delights young readers.

Miss Warner lived in Putnam, Connecticut, until her death in 1979. During her lifetime, she received hundreds of letters from girls and boys telling her how much they liked her books.